Under the Star

A CHRISTMAS COUNTING STORY

Jane Yolen

Illustrated by Vlasta van Kampen

Under the star, under the star,

One angel sees a manger afar.

Under the star, under the star,

Two shepherds see a manger afar.

Under the star, under the star,

Three wise men see a manger afar.

Under the star, under the star,

Four goats see a manger afar.

Under the star, under the star,

Five sheep see a manger afar.

Under the star, under the star,

Six cows see a manger afar.

Under the star, under the star,

Seven horses see a manger afar.

Under the star, under the star,

Eight mothers see a manger afar.

Under the star, under the star,

Nine fathers see a manger afar.

Under the star, under the star,

Ten children see a manger afar.

They all crowd in heedless of danger,

To see the star shine in the manger.

To Bob and Debby Harris, with love.—JY

For my dear friend Marie Matte. For your love, care, encouragement and sharing throughout the creative process of this special book, I thank you with all my heart.—VvK

Library and Archives Canada Cataloguing in Publication data is available upon request.

The publisher gratefully acknowledges the support of the Canada Council for the Arts and the Ontario Arts Council for its publishing program. We acknowledge the support of the Government of Ontario through the Ontario Media Development Corporation's Ontario Book Initiative.

We acknowledge the financial support of the Government of Canada through the Book Publishing Industry Development Program (BPIDP) for our publishing activities.

KPk is an imprint of
Key Porter Books Limited
Six Adelaide Street East, Tenth Floor
Toronto, Ontario
Canada M5C 1H6

www.keyporter.com

Design: Martin Gould

Printed and bound in China

09 10 11 12 13 5 4 3 2 1